Andy's Pocketknife

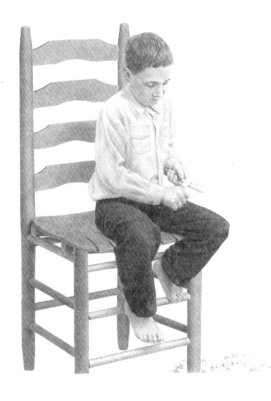

Andy's Pocketknife

By Dorcas R. Mast
Illustrated by Peter Balholm

Rod and Staff Publishers, Inc.
P.O. Box 3, Hwy. 172
Crockett, Kentucky 41413
Telephone 606-522-4348

To my grandfather,
Andrew D. Stutzman.

Thank you for a heritage
of real-life stories!

Rod and Staff Publishers, Inc.
P.O. Box 3, Hwy. 172
Crockett, Kentucky 41413

Printed in U.S.A.

ISBN 978-07399-2581-2
Catalog no. 2104

Andy's Pocketknife

Andy looked at his pocketknife. It was a wonderful knife. It had a shiny blade with a sharp edge. It had a fine, shiny handle. The handle was smooth and cool in his hand.

Andy liked his knife. It was the best thing he owned. It was very special.

Father had given the knife to Andy one day when he had come home from town. He had said, "All boys need a pocketknife, Andy. Here is a pocketknife for you. Take good care of it, and it will last you for a long, long time."

After that, Andy carried his pocketknife everywhere.

When he went to the barn, his pocketknife went along. The string on the feed bag got twisted into a knot. Then Andy used his pocketknife to cut the string.

When it was time to walk back to the pasture for the cows, he waded into the muddy creek to cut a branch from a willow tree that leaned over the water.

"Better be careful, Andy," said his big brother Marion. "If you dropped your pocketknife now, you'd never find it again."

"Oh, I won't drop it," said Andy. He
flipped his knife shut and put it in his
pocket.

When Andy and his brothers took a walk in the woods, he used his knife to cut his initials in a big white sycamore tree.

His knife slipped a little, and the blade nipped his other hand.

"Ouch!" said Andy. His finger was bleeding. He wiped the blood on his pants.

"Better be careful, Andy," said his big brother Roman. "Next thing you'll cut off your finger."

"Oh, I won't," said Andy. He finished cutting his initials, but he was more careful after that.

When Rover got a big mat of burs stuck in the fur behind his ears, Andy used his knife to cut them off.

"Better be careful, Andy," said big brother Henry. "Don't cut into his skin."

"Oh, I won't," said Andy. He tossed the burs into the grass, wiped his knife on his pants, and slid it into his pocket.

When Elizabeth wanted him to pick some apples for her, he took his knife along.

"Now mind, Andy," Elizabeth called after him. "I want apples off the Baldwin tree, because I am making pies."

"Oh, I know," said Andy.

He poked around in the orchard. He liked the crooked old trees and the long, sweet grass under them. Carefully he chose the ripest Baldwins he could find. He put them into a burlap sack.

"A-a-andy," he heard Elizabeth calling from far away.

Uh-oh. Elizabeth was getting impatient. But Andy hadn't gotten an apple for himself yet. And he didn't want a Baldwin. He wanted an Orange Pippin.

Most of the pippins were already gone from the tree. But Andy saw a big one hanging high up in the tree. He'd have to climb up and get it.

He picked the apple and cut it in half
with his pocketknife. He took one bite. It
was sweet and spicy, just the way apples
were supposed to be.

"A-a-andy," he heard Elizabeth call again. "I'm wa-a-aiting."

Andy quickly flipped his knife shut and slid it into his pocket. He put half of his apple into his pocket with the knife. The other half he held in his teeth.

He slid down out of the tree. "Ouch!" he mumbled through his apple. "Now I've got a splinter in my hand."

He got out his pocketknife and used it to scrape the splinter out. Really, this

pocketknife was becoming his best helper, next to Rover.

When he had some time to play in the afternoon, he used his knife to carve the piece of willow branch into a whistle.

"Now don't leave a mess on the porch please, Andy," said Anna, frowning at the shavings on the porch floor.

"Oh, I won't," said Andy. He used his bare feet to push the shavings off the porch into the grass.

When it was time to leave for church on Sunday, Andy picked up his knife. He looked at the smooth, shiny handle. He knew that Father would not want him to take the knife to church.

But Andy thought that he would be lonely without his knife. His knife was such a good helper. He would not look at the knife during church. Quickly he slid the knife into his pocket.

Andy and most of his family crowded into their surrey. It was quite a tight fit. They did not have room for everyone, so Henry and Roman had to walk to church.

Father clicked the lines, and Pet lifted her feet gaily. The surrey wheels flung off sparkles of sunshine.

After a while, Andy got bored. He wiggled forward enough so that he could get his hand into his pocket.

"What *are* you doing?" Elizabeth asked. "You're wrinkling up my dress."

Andy didn't answer. He got his knife from his pocket and wiggled back again. He was careful not to wrinkle Elizabeth's dress, although he could not see how it could help being wrinkled anyway, so jammed were they in the surrey.

Andy held his knife. He looked at the smooth, shiny handle. He flipped the blade open to see if it was clean.

On his other side, Marion was looking
too. He was frowning. "Father," Marion
said, "Andy brought his knife along to
church."

"Son, you know you shouldn't bring your pocketknife to church," Father said from the front seat. "Why did you bring it along?"

Andy did not know what to say. He thought for a bit. "I wanted to take it with me," he said. "I wasn't going to look at it during church."

"We are going to church to worship God," said Father. "God wants us to listen to His Word. He wants us to think about Him. He does not want us to think about our pocketknives.

"When we get to church, you must leave your pocketknife in the surrey."

"But what if someone would see it and steal it?" asked Andy. He did not want to leave his pocketknife in the surrey.

"Perhaps," said Father, "you should have thought of that sooner."

Andy did not say anything more. He knew that Father would not change his mind. He also knew that he should not have brought his knife along to church.

When everyone had gotten out of the surrey, Andy sadly put his smooth, shiny knife onto the seat.

He walked sadly into the church house. His pocket felt empty without his knife.

After church, Andy and his family went to their friends' house for dinner. Andy held his knife in his hand the whole way. He was glad that no one had seen his knife and taken it.

When Andy climbed out of the surrey, he slid his knife into his pocket.

"Better leave your knife in the surrey," said Roman. "If you and your friends play the way you usually do, it might fall out of your pocket. Then you'd lose it for good."

"Oh, I won't," said Andy. He hurried after Father and Mother. He wanted to find Jacob. They would have a fine time together. He would show Jacob his new knife.

Andy and Jacob did have a fine time that afternoon. It didn't seem long at all before Father called to say it was time to go home.

Andy and Jacob ran to the house. Father and Mother were still talking, so Andy leaned against the doorframe while he waited.

Father kept on talking, and Andy became bored.

He looked at the doorframe beside him. It had a hole in it where the latch of the door fitted in. He put his finger into the hole. He wondered what was down in the hole, but his finger didn't reach very far. Did the hole have a bottom?

Father was still talking. So Andy got out his knife. He poked it into the hole. He still couldn't feel anything.

Suddenly the smooth, shiny knife slipped out of his fingers. It slipped down into the hole and disappeared. *Plunk.*

Andy's mouth dropped open. His knife! His knife had fallen into the hole! It had fallen the whole way to the bottom of the wall!

He could *never* get it out.

Several days later, Andy found Father working in the barn.

"Father," he said sadly, "all boys need a pocketknife. My pocket is lonely without one."

"I know, son," Father said. He put his hand on Andy's shoulder. "But you know that we do not have much money. You know that I cannot buy you another knife right away."

Andy swallowed hard. "Couldn't we somehow get the knife out of the wall?" he asked.

"I don't know how unless we would take the doorframe apart," said Father. "And perhaps that would ruin the wall or the doorframe. We cannot ask Jacob's family to do that."

Andy nodded. He looked down at the floor and pushed a few pieces of hay together in a pile with his bare foot.

"Is there anything that you think you can learn from this?" Father asked kindly.

Andy nodded slowly. "I should not have taken my knife to church," he said.

"That's right," said Father. "If you had left your knife at home where it belonged, you would not have lost your knife Sunday afternoon.

"And do you remember that when we got to Jacob's house, Roman suggested that you should leave your knife in the surrey so that it wouldn't get lost? Then you said, 'Oh, I won't.' You've been a little too cocky, Andy — a little too sure of yourself. Perhaps the next time someone gives you some advice, you would do well to listen.

"Sometime we will get you another knife," said Father. "But not for a while."

Andy soberly picked up a scoop shovel. He knew that Father was right. It was his own fault that he had lost his knife.

Many, many years later, a surprising thing happened to Andy. He had become a preacher by then. And one Sunday, he preached a sermon at another church.

When church was over, an old man came up to Andy. "Do you know who I am?" he asked.

"Jacob!" said Andy. "Of course I know who you are. I haven't seen you for a very long time."

"You're right!" said Jacob. "It has been a long time."

Jacob reached into his pocket. "I've got something for you, Andy."

He pulled something from his pocket. It was smooth and not very shiny. He put it in Andy's hand.

"What!" said Andy. He turned it over and over. He held it up to the light. "It's my knife! How did you ever get my knife?"

Jacob chuckled. "I still live in the old farmhouse where I lived when I was a boy," he said. "Not long ago, we were remodeling the house. We had to tear some walls out.

"I still remembered that your knife was in that wall. So when my sons tore that wall out, I told them to find the knife. Sure enough, there it was!"

"Well, well," said Andy. He looked at his knife. He felt the smooth handle that was not shiny anymore. He smiled to think that he had gotten his knife back after fifty years.

The two old men smiled at each other. Then Andy leaned forward and shook his finger in Jacob's face. "You know what?" he said. "This little knife taught me one of the best lessons I ever learned!"